PET QUEST

JENNY McLACHLAN
ILLUSTRATED BY SARAH HOYLE

BLOOMSBURY EDUCATION

LONDON   OXFORD   NEW YORK   NEW DELHI   SYDNEY

BLOOMSBURY EDUCATION
Bloomsbury Publishing Plc
50 Bedford Square, London, WC1B 3DP, UK

BLOOMSBURY, BLOOMSBURY EDUCATION and the Diana logo are
trademarks of Bloomsbury Publishing Plc

First published in Great Britain in 2018 by Bloomsbury Publishing Plc

A catalogue record for this book is available from the British Library

ISBN: PB: 978-1-4729-5192-2; ePDF: 978-1-4729-5191-5; ePub: 978-1-4729-5189-2

2 4 6 8 10 9 7 5 3 1

Printed and bound in China by Leo Paper Products, Heshan, Guangdong

All papers used by Bloomsbury Publishing Plc are natural, recyclable products from wood grown
in well managed forests. The manufacturing processes conform to the environmental regulations
of the country of origin.

To find out more about our authors and books visit www.bloomsbury.com
and sign up for our newsletters

Chapter One

One sunny afternoon, Harvey was at the park with his dad. Harvey saw a yellow dog swimming in the pond.

He saw a spotty dog catching
a ball in its mouth.

On the way home, he saw a tabby cat rolling on its back. Harvey tickled its tummy.

"Dad," said Harvey, "can we get a pet?"

"No way," said Dad. "Our flat is too small for a pet. There's hardly room for you, me and your mum."

"We could get a small pet," said
Harvey. "What about a hamster?"
But Dad shook his head. "Sorry,
Harvey. If we move house, you can
get a pet."

Well, Harvey knew that was never going to happen!

Chapter Two

On the way home, Dad stopped to chat to a friend. Harvey had a look for a tiny pet that would fit in their flat.

Soon he found a large black slug. Perfect! Carefully, he put the slug in his pocket.

When they got back to the flat, Harvey looked for a home for his pet slug.

His toy car was no good. The slug
could get out of the windows.

His lunch box was the right size but it
looked a bit dark.

Then Harvey found the perfect place for the slug: the glass Mum kept by her bed. He put the slug in the glass and put a book on top.

"I'm going to call you
Slimy," he said to the slug.
Harvey watched Slimy
moving up and down
the glass.

Then he went off to do some drawing. He was doing such a good picture of a monster that he forgot all about Slimy.

Then he heard a scream coming from Mum and Dad's bedroom. Mum had found Slimy!

"Our flat is too small for pets!" Mum said. Then she took Slimy downstairs and put him in a flower bed.

Chapter Three

Harvey missed Slimy. The next time he went to the park he looked for a new pet.

If the flat was too small for a slug,
this pet would have to be even smaller.
He found the perfect pet under the
slide: a spider.

It was smaller than Slimy, but big for a spider. Harvey could see the hairs on its body and eight big legs.

Harvey decided it was
probably a boy.
"I'm going to call
you Hairy," he said
to the spider.
Then he put
Hairy in his
empty water
bottle and took
him home.

It was hard finding somewhere to keep Hairy because he was good at escaping. In the end, Harvey put him in the bath. The sides were too steep for Hairy to climb out.

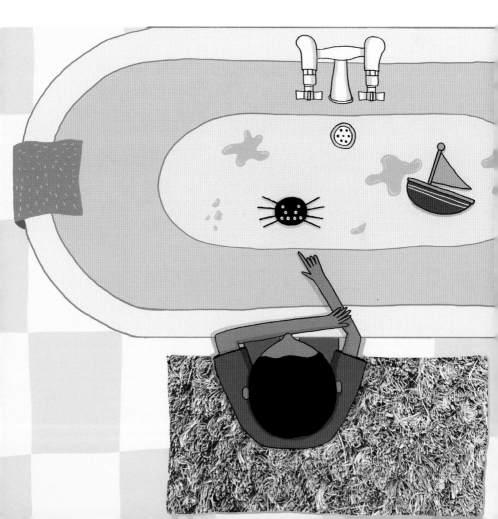

It was Dad who found Hairy.
His scream was even louder
than Mum's.

Harvey ran into the bathroom. "Don't
hurt Hairy!" he yelled. "He's my pet."
"Our flat is too small for pets!" said
Dad. Then he put Hairy in a cup
and let him go outside.

Chapter Four

Harvey found his next pet in the school playground. It was an ant.

It was teeny weeny. There was definitely room for an ant in their flat. Harvey called the ant Teeny and decided she was a girl. He put Teeny in his sandwich box and took her home.

Teeny needed a
tiny place to live.
Harvey's mum had
a special soap that
no one else was
allowed to use.
She kept the soap
in a plastic pot.
Harvey decided
the pot was just the
right size for Teeny.

Harvey was playing with Lego when he
heard the scream. "Harvey!" yelled his
mum. "Our flat is too small for pets!"

Harvey felt sad. What pet was smaller than an ant? Was he going to have to give up looking for a pet?

Chapter Five

"I know what will cheer you up," said Mum. "I will take you to see Uncle Joe. He's just got a new kitten."

The kitten did cheer Harvey up. He was black with white spots. Harvey showed him how to chase a ribbon. Harvey helped to feed him. Harvey stroked his soft paws.

And that is how he found
Jumpy. Jumpy was a flea
that was living on the
kitten. It jumped from
the kitten right onto
Harvey's arm.

Harvey put his hand over the flea and kept it there. When it was time to go home he wouldn't move his hand.

"You need to put your coat on," said Mum.
"I don't want to," said Harvey.
"I'm not cold."
Mum shrugged. "Suit yourself," she said.

She wanted to
get home quickly
because Gran was
coming to tea.

Harvey walked all the way home holding tight to his arm. It made his arm ache. His mum kept giving him funny looks, but he never let go. Finally, they got home.

Chapter Six

It was hard finding a safe place for
Jumpy. The flea was just so small.
In the end, Harvey put Jumpy under
a glass on the table.

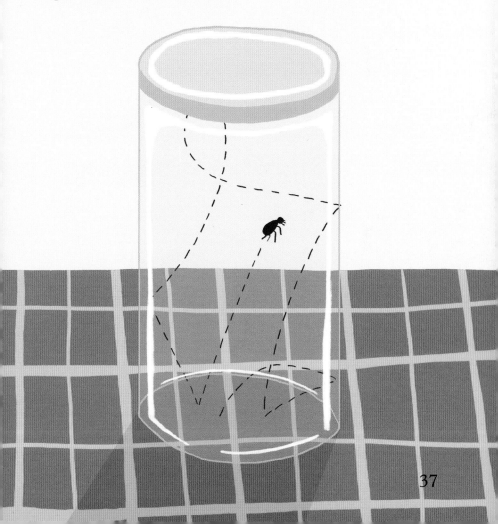

He watched the flea through the glass until the doorbell rang.

"Gran's here!" called Mum.

Gran had brought a chocolate cake and a sticker book for Harvey. He had so much fun eating cake and doing his stickers that he forgot about Jumpy.

Then he heard Gran say, "Can I have a glass of water?"
Harvey looked up. There was only one glass on the table and Jumpy was in it!

Gran picked up the glass. Jumpy flew out and landed on Gran's hand. Then Jumpy jumped up her arm and did a giant leap on to her specs.

Gran screamed. Mum screamed.
Harvey yelled, "Don't hurt Jumpy!"

Mum looked at Harvey. She started to laugh. "You really, *really* want a pet, don't you?"

Harvey
nodded.
"I want
a pet more
than anything
in the world,"
he said.

Gran carried her glasses to the window and put Jumpy on the window sill. Then they all put on their coats and got into the car. They drove to a pet shop.

Harvey was allowed to choose a
hamster. He picked the smallest one.
She was yellow and had soft hair.
Harvey called her Fluffy.

Fluffy was bigger than a flea, an ant, a spider and a slug.

Fluffy was the perfect pet for the flat.

Fluffy was the perfect pet for Harvey.